W9-DGG-561

Heroes

Jyotirmayee Mohapatra
Advocate for India's Young Women

Adam Woog

KIDHAVEN PRESS
An imprint of Thomson Gale, a part of The Thomson Corporation

THOMSON

GALE

Detroit • New York • San Francisco
New Haven, Conn. • Waterville, Maine • London

THOMSON

GALE

*Thanks to Bharti Kirchner, Sheila Kinkade,
and Christina Macy for their help.*

LIBRARY OF CONGRESS CATALOGING-IN-PUBLICATION DATA

Woog, Adam, 1953–
    Jyotirmayee Mohapatra: advocate for India's young women / by Adam Woog.
      p. cm. -- (Young heroes)
    Includes bibliographical references and index.
    ISBN-13: 978-0-7377-3611-3 (hard covers : alk. paper)
    ISBN-10: 0-7377-3611-9 (hard covers : alk. paper)
    1. Mohapatra, Jyotirmayee, 1978– . 2. Feminists—India—Biography —Juvenile literature. 3. Women social reformers—India—Biography —Juvenile literature. 4. Young volunteers—India—Biography—Juvenile literature. 5. Social action—India—Case studies—Juvenile literature. 6. Girls—India—Societies and clubs—Juvenile literature.   I. Title. II. Series: Young heroes (San Diego, Calif.)
HQ1742.5.M64W66 2006
                                   305.420954—dc22

Printed in the United States of America

Contents

Chapter One

Introducing Jyoti

When she was a teenager, Jyotirmayee Mohapatra (Joe-teer-maa-yee Ma-ha-pa-tra) was, in many ways, a typical young woman growing up in a **rural** village in India. However, Jyoti (as most people call her) was unusual in an important way. She stood up for herself and others in the face of injustice and cruelty.

In traditional Indian society, especially in rural areas like Jyoti's, girls and women lead very difficult lives. They often do not have the same rights as boys and men. For example, they often cannot go to school or hold jobs when they grow up. Often, they are treated harshly or even beaten by their fathers or husbands.

But Jyoti was different. She was not content with the way things were. She became a leader in fighting for the rights of girls and women.

The Meena Club

She formed a club, the Meena Club, named for a girl in a famous series of stories. The club gave

Jyoti and others a chance to discuss their problems and find solutions. But the "Meena Girls" in the club were not content with just talking about issues. They also brought about change in their village.

The success of the Meena Club helped the whole community, not just the girls and women. This was because the whole village became involved in bettering itself. Jyoti states, "We believe that unity is our strength,

Girls and women in rural India often do not have the same rights as boys and men.

so we try to involve the entire community. Our goal is to create a child-friendly society."[1]

The idea behind the Meena Club spread quickly and widely. Many other girls and young women in villages around Jyoti's formed their own clubs. Today, there are hundreds of Meena Clubs and thousands of "Meena Girls" all across Jyoti's part of India.

Expressing Themselves

Belonging to the Meena Clubs has helped these young women become stronger and more self-confident. It has given them the strength to fight for their rights. Some of

Meena Clubs throughout India have helped girls and young women envision a brighter future for themselves.

them wrote about themselves, "Meena Clubs gave these almost forgotten girls a way to express themselves."[2]

The Meena Girls have helped themselves by becoming more confident and self-assured in their abilities. They have proved to themselves that they can accomplish something really good and important. This gives them the strength to tackle bigger projects. As the members of the Mantapada Meena Club wrote about a typical Meena Girl, "She is now confident of a different world in the near future."[3]

Jyoti agrees. She adds that all young people, not just girls, have a great opportunity to create change. She believes that they need to get ready for the serious job of taking care of society. Jyoti says, "I believe that change comes from the power of youth. Youth are in the forefront, because they ask questions that no one else dares to ask."[4]

Because Jyoti was the founder and leader of the original Meena Club, she has become a symbol of the ongoing effort to improve the lives of women and girls in India. Recently, as Jyoti's fame has grown, **activists** around the world have also come to know about her. Her bravery, imagination, and determination inspire people everywhere who are working to improve society.

Jyoti Goes to School

Jyoti was born in 1978 and raised in a village called Mantapada. Mantapada is in the state of Orissa, in the northeast part of India. It is on the coast of Orissa, beside a huge body of water called the Bay of Bengal.

Jyoti's village was a typical rural Indian village in many ways. One of its typical characteristics was a lack of good schools. It was very difficult for young people growing up there to get a good education, especially girls, and many children in Mantapada barely went to school at all.

But Jyoti was not a typical child. She was very bright, and she was eager to get an education. Jyoti was also luckier than many other girls in her situation. Her parents allowed her to finish high school, even though most of her friends did not.

Jyoti's parents also helped her mature in other ways. Her mother was an especially good role model. She was a member of the village council, the group that makes decisions for the community as a whole. Watching her mother, Jyoti realized that women could be the equals of men. She says, "I saw that it was possible, as a woman, to play a role in society."[5]

On to the University

After Jyoti graduated from high school, she wanted to continue her education. She wanted to study political science, the study of how politics and governments work. Jyoti's dream was to use this education to help people—in her village and beyond—to lead better lives.

However, at first her parents were not sure that Jyoti should go to a university. They argued that it was in another town, far away from their village. They worried about her safety there, because she would be alone with no family nearby to protect her.

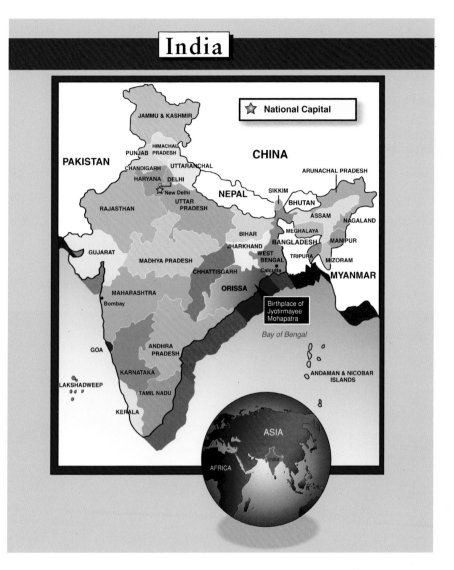

India

- National Capital

JAMMU & KASHMIR

HIMACHAL PRADESH

PUNJAB

CHANDIGARH

PAKISTAN

HARYANA DELHI

UTTARANCHAL

New Delhi

CHINA

ARUNACHAL PRADESH

RAJASTHAN

UTTAR PRADESH

NEPAL

SIKKIM

BHUTAN

ASSAM

NAGALAND

MEGHALAYA

MANIPUR

BIHAR

JHARKHAND

BANGLADESH

GUJARAT

MADHYA PRADESH

WEST BENGAL

TRIPURA

MIZORAM

CHHATTISGARH

Calcutta

MYANMAR

MAHARASHTRA

Bombay

ORISSA

Birthplace of Jyotirmayee Mohapatra

Bay of Bengal

GOA

ANDHRA PRADESH

KARNATAKA

LAKSHADWEEP

TAMIL NADU

ANDAMAN & NICOBAR ISLANDS

KERALA

ASIA

AFRICA

India

They also knew that women are expected to marry in their society, but they worried that no man would want to marry Jyoti if she was too educated. According to the customs of traditional Indian society, it is not proper for a woman to have a better education than her husband has. Jyoti's parents were afraid that she would be lonely in her old age if she never married.

9

However, Jyoti insisted on continuing her education. She knew that it was a necessary part of pursuing her dreams. Fortunately, she succeeded in convincing her parents.

Beginning to Address the Problems

At the university, Jyoti began to learn more about the many serious social problems that face India, especially its girls and women. She also began to think about specific ways to help the women and children in Mantapada.

Unlike many young women in India, these women are attending university.

When she was nineteen, during a break in her studies, Jyoti returned home to Mantapada. She wanted to do something more than just study. Jyoti wanted to find a project that would improve living conditions for people there.

She began by going around the village with a few friends. They knocked on every door and talked to everyone they could. They wanted to organize a group of women and girls to meet informally to discuss problems and issues.

The first meeting was a little disappointing. Only five people showed up. However, each one of these people was eager to talk about her life, and to think about ways of improving it. They were all glad to come to the meeting, because it was a safe place for them to talk without fear of being punished. This safe feeling was a good first step, Jyoti says: "Part of change is being able to have honest talk."[6]

Word spread quickly around the village that the meeting had gone well. The second gathering was therefore very different—more than 60 women and girls came! The group continued to discuss some of the problems they faced—and to think about solutions for some of them.

Two

The Problems

Many of the problems that Jyoti and her friends discussed are still serious problems in India today. For example, much of India suffers from **poverty**, poor **sanitation**, and scarce health facilities. Such problems, of course, can affect anyone—male or female, child or adult. But girls and women tend to be affected the most because of their lower status in India's traditional society.

Poverty is perhaps India's most serious problem. Although it is making rapid improvements, India is overall a poor country. The problem of poverty is especially serious in Orissa, the state where Mantapada, Jyoti's home village, is located. Orissa is one of the poorest regions in India. It has the highest rate for infant deaths in India, and the lowest number of doctors per person. About 80 percent of the homes there have no electricity or running water.

Many other problems stem from poverty. Chief among these is hunger. In places like Orissa, finding enough food (or making enough money) to support a family can be very difficult. As a result, people often do not have enough to eat.

Bad housing also stems from poverty. Many people are so poor that they are homeless. If they do have houses, the buildings are typically little more than shacks. Many do not have electricity, inside toilets, or running water. In some regions, such as Orissa, most of the houses are this way.

Problems for Everyone

A big problem connected to poverty, hunger, and bad housing is the question of health. If people cannot eat properly, or do not have the money for medicine, their health suffers. A typical village cannot afford to keep

A young mother living in a slum in India comforts her child.

Children play in an open sewer in Mumbai, India, putting their health at risk.

its water wells and other public facilities maintained and cleaned properly, which adds to the health risk.

In such situations, people can easily get sick. When they do, they typically cannot receive proper health care, because there are few doctors. Sometimes health workers from aid agencies can travel to poor villages, but there are never enough to go around and help everyone.

The Problems of Women and Girls

Because of all of these problems, life can be very hard for any poor person in India. But it is especially hard for people who live in rural villages like Mantapada. And it is perhaps hardest of all for the girls and women of these rural villages, where old traditions and customs are still strong.

Traditional Indian society considers girls to be unequal to boys. Girls are often neglected or treated cruelly. For example, they might be denied proper medicine or given inferior food, while a boy would get much better care and food.

The problem runs even deeper. Families often consider girls to be bad luck and burdensome. To get rid of

A baby girl plays alone in a garbage bin in a poor area of India.

them, parents often force girls to marry when they are very young—sometimes as young as eight or ten. Often girls are forced into marriages with men they barely know, or who are much older. Many become mothers while they are still teenagers.

Burdens

Another issue connected to marriage is the tradition of paying a **dowry**. According to this ancient custom, when a girl gets married her father pays cash, goods, or property to the groom. Officially, paying a dowry is illegal in India. However, it is still a common practice, especially in rural communities.

The tradition of paying dowries means that girls are financial burdens on poor families, who must pay large amounts to make sure their daughters get married. If a family cannot afford a dowry, a daughter will have to stay at home and will still be a financial burden. Since many girls do not work, their families will continue to pay for their upkeep.

If girls do work outside the home, sometimes they must start when they are very young. This practice is called **child labor**. About one-fourth of all the children in India work in factories or at similar adult jobs. Many children work in such terrible conditions that their health is permanently affected.

Furthermore, sometimes infant girls are killed before they grow up. This is illegal, and the Indian government is trying hard to stop it from happening. However, these deaths frequently occur anyway, be-

A young woman from a wealthy family sits in front of the dowry that will be offered to her future husband.

cause some families are so poor that they simply cannot afford to raise daughters. Sometimes mothers or grandmothers are the ones who kill their infant girls, because the adults cannot stand to think of their daughters suffering as much as they themselves have suffered.

Because of neglect, bad working conditions, and infant death, the death rate among girls in India is much higher than it is for boys. About one-fourth of Indian girls do not live past the age of fifteen. Even if they do live, they are likely to suffer from **chronic** illnesses because of poor medical care or bad nutrition.

Abuse

Still another serious problem, for all children but especially for girls, is **child abuse**. Like all countries, India has laws designed to find and punish adults who abuse children. However, these laws are often not strictly enforced in rural communities.

Furthermore, the standards are different for girls than for boys. For example, police officers are likely to arrest a parent who is beating a son. However, the same authorities might not think it necessary to make an arrest if the child is a girl.

Abuse often is forced not just on girls but on grown women. Sometimes this takes the form of what is called **bride torture** or dowry torture. This happens when a groom harms his bride in order to force the bride's family to pay more dowry money.

Many cases of dowry torture have been reported in India. In some of the most extreme cases, grooms permanently disfigure or even kill their brides because the dowries they received were too small. It is estimated that about 5,000 Indian brides are killed annually in dowry-related deaths.

Education

Still another problem in rural India is access to education. Villages are typically too poor to maintain proper school buildings, buy supplies, or hire teachers. If they

Instead of going to school, millions of children in India must work to help support their families.

go to school, children must frequently walk long distances to larger towns. And it is estimated that almost one-half of the 200 million children and young people in India do not attend school at all.

Girls have an especially difficult time getting an education. It is estimated that more than half of the girls and women in India are **illiterate**. They have not even learned the basics of reading and writing.

This is because traditional Indian society teaches that educating girls beyond cooking and cleaning is a waste of time. According to this way of thinking, a girl has two options. She can stay at home after she grows up to care for her parents, or she can get married and then cook and clean house for her husband and children.

Doing Something

These are just some of the worst problems facing the girls and women of India. Jyoti witnessed such problems

This school holds lessons outdoors because there is not enough classroom space.

every day when she was young. She recalls, "My growing up was no different from other girls and women, unprotected and suppressed [silenced]. Children were invisible, and women were not treated properly."[7]

So Jyoti and her friends had a lot to talk about when they decided to hold their first discussion meetings together. Those first meetings continued to draw more and more interested people, and the group decided to meet regularly.

Chapter Three

The Meena Club Is Born

Jyoti and her friends called their group the Meena Club. The name came from a series of fictional stories about an energetic, curious, and intelligent girl named Meena who was not afraid to fight for her rights. UNICEF, the United Nations Children's Fund, created Meena to help educate people about the problems of girls.

The agency first created animated cartoons for television. But millions of Indians have no TV, so UNICEF workers sometimes traveled to perform plays and puppet shows. In this way, even the most isolated villages could meet Meena.

Meena

Each Meena story illustrated a different problem. Among the topics were education, first aid for babies, and good health habits. Other subjects were child marriage and school bullies.

The Meena stories showed why solving these problems can be good for everyone. For example, in one episode Meena is not allowed to go to school. But Meena secretly persuades a friend (a boy) to show her what he is learning in school.

One day, Meena is practicing math by counting her father's chickens. She notices that one is missing and spots a thief running away. Meena alerts her father and the thief is caught. Her family realizes that math skills are important for everyone.

"Meenas in Real Life"

Meena became very popular in India. She represented the hope that women and girls could be given more power and respect. Now there is an annual Meena Day

The Meena character was created to help promote the rights of girls.

in India, part of a big annual celebration called Girl Child Week.

Jyoti first saw Meena in 1999 when a social group in her village, Nature's Club, showed the cartoons. This was at about the same time that Jyoti and her friends were starting to meet for their discussion groups.

Jyoti and the other girls loved Meena, and they decided to name their group in her honor. They knew that Meena was fictional, but they also knew that her problems were the problems of real girls. Jyoti recalls, "When we saw those . . . films, we thought: why can't our girls be Meenas in real life?"[8]

Meena Clubs have given girls confidence and helped them feel better about themselves.

Building the Club

After their first few meetings, the Meena Girls, as they called themselves, realized that they were not satisfied with just talking. They wanted to be activists and do positive, productive things for their village.

At first, the Meena Girls were not encouraged or taken seriously by the adults in Mantapada. Many of the grown-ups did not think their daughters should be activists. Often, family members and others, such as village leaders and police officers, blocked the Meena Girls when they tried to meet or work.

However, gradually the girls gained respect. They did this by being patient, persistent, and polite, persuading adults without offending them. Jyoti says, "We realized that . . . problems cannot be resolved with aggression, that it helps if we are soft-spoken and nonthreatening."[9]

Word spread, and many girls in neighboring villages were inspired to form their own Meena Clubs. The original Meena Girls, including Jyoti, supported these other clubs and helped them get started. They told them how their club was improving their village and helping them feel better about themselves.

Helping Young Women

Sometimes the projects of the Meena Girls helped just one person at a time. For example, in the village of Kandia, a young girl had been badly abused. Everyone knew who was responsible, but the police did nothing. The local Meena Club staged a protest campaign and the police were forced to take action.

25

Another example took place in the village of Matia, when three men attacked a girl as she returned home. She ran away, but while she was running she lost some books and some heavy anklets with bells that are used for dancing. For a poor family like hers, these were serious losses.

Members of the local Meena Club met with village leaders and persuaded them to punish the attackers. The leaders made the attackers pay for the lost articles. Afterward, the attackers felt so unwelcome in the village that they moved away.

Disasters

Sometimes the Meena Clubs work to help all people, not just girls and women. One example came in 1999, when a massive storm called a super **cyclone** struck the coast of Orissa. It caused terrible damage, killing about 10,000 people and leaving at least 1 million homeless.

Meena Clubs all across the region aided victims in many ways. They helped run shelters for homeless people. They pitched in to keep drinking water clean and collect garbage before disease could spread. And they visited remote villages to make sure that food and supplies were being distributed properly.

The government of Orissa welcomed the Meena Girls' help during this crisis. One official said, "The Meena Groups have helped us in achieving results [and] we would like to extend [their aid] as a government-sponsored project."[10]

Orissa residents survey the damage from a cyclone that killed thousands of people and left many more homeless.

Other Projects

Since then, Meena Clubs have often come to the aid of people in need. For example, they helped the United Nations organize a program for poor farming families.

The clubs were given money to buy seeds, **fertilizer**, and **pesticide**, then distributed them to farmers. About 500 acres of new crops were created. The clubs then asked the families to repay them after the harvest, and half of this money was saved for future projects.

Meena Girls have also helped complete many large repair projects, such as when roads are washed out. In Mantapada, for example, a contractor was hired to fix a road, but his work was slow and poor quality. The Meena Club threatened a hunger strike, and the contractor was forced

Meena Club members have helped poor farming families by providing them with seeds, fertilizer, and pesticides.

to finish. In appreciation, the village's residents built the club a permanent meeting house.

In Malisahada, meanwhile, sanitation was especially bad. The village's leaders had not allowed girls to organize a club there. About 50 Meena Girls from other villages traveled to Malisahada and began cleaning its garbage and drains. The villagers were inspired to finish the job themselves. After that, girls were allowed to form a Meena Club there and could use a community hall that had previously been off-limits to women.

These are just a few of the many accomplishments of the Meena Clubs. There have been many more. And there will be even more in the future.

Work for the Future

Since its early days, the Meena Club network has continued to grow. Today, more than 300 Meena Clubs and about 11,000 Meena Girls are active across Orissa. Jyoti says, "This idea is an idea whose time was ripe. The Meena Clubs have spread so rapidly because there is a great need for this kind of activity."[11]

For several years, Jyoti was well known only around her home state of Orissa. Few people had heard of her outside the region until recently. Then, on October 3, 2004, when she was 26 years old, Jyoti was presented with an important honor.

She was one of a group of young people who received that year's International Youth Action Net Award. It was presented by the International Youth Foundation of Baltimore, Maryland. These young people were honored because each had done something important to change the world for the better.

Jyoti's tireless activism has helped improve the lives of young people throughout India.

The Award

The presentation ceremony took place in Buenos Aires, Argentina. Jyoti was very excited to go. Before she traveled there, she had never been outside India. (She still lives in her remote farming village of Mantapada with her family, which includes four sisters and a younger brother.)

In Argentina, Jyoti spent five days meeting with other award winners. These young people working to improve life in their own countries made a huge impact on Jyoti. She said, "I now feel that I am not alone working to create social change. . . . I feel energized [and] part of a bigger community."[12]

After the ceremony, Jyoti returned to her village. A huge crowd of girls and young women met her there to congratulate her. Jyoti commented, "There has been a flow of

30

greetings from all my Meena-mates and people have made a beeline for my house ever since I returned home."[13]

Jyoti felt honored to receive the award. However, she said that others in her village also deserved recognition. She said, "I dedicate this international recognition to each resident here, [because without their] support the Meena volunteers would have remained unknown."[14]

What You Can Do

One of the important lessons Jyoti learned from her experience was that anyone can become an activist. It is an important part of being a good citizen and a good neighbor. There are many things that kids can do to become

Because of the clubs Jyoti started, many girls are experiencing positive changes in their daily lives.

activists like Jyoti. A good first step is to join an organization that supports a worthy cause.

For example, many organizations are devoted to the rights of young people, both in America and worldwide. One is Voices of Youth (VOY), which is sponsored by UNICEF. VOY's Web site has excellent suggestions for things young people can do to help make the world better.

Another good step is to start a club of your own. Such a club does not have to have formal memberships, elected officers, or any age limits, Jyoti feels. She says, "A ten-year-old can also be a **mentor** [to others], and can have equal standing within the group. This is what builds leaders and confidence."[15]

Getting Involved

A club can meet anywhere—in someone's living room, maybe, or in school after classes. Its members can raise money for its expenses in many ways, such as by holding a bake sale or organizing a garage sale. A club might not need much money, however. A simple discussion group, after all, costs almost nothing.

There are also many ways to become a local activist, right in your own community. Jyoti says, "Every place you stand, there are enough problems and needs to be addressed. So don't look someplace else. The challenge is right in front of you: your family, your community, on your street."[16]

For instance, some young people in Seattle, Washington, knew about a big vacant lot that was going to

Children of any age can start a club to support a worthy cause.

waste. By writing e-mails, talking to people, and sending a petition to the city, they convinced authorities to turn it into a skateboard park that all kids could enjoy. Much of the work to make it a park was volunteer labor that the young people organized themselves.

Another example was a benefit concert held by two fifth-grade students. They wanted to raise money to help a friend who had recently been adopted from Ethiopia. Their whole class was raising enough money to bring her brothers and sisters to America as well.

The two students took their saxophones to a music festival where anyone could play and "pass the hat" for donations. They made a big sign that said that any money they made was going to a good cause. When they saw this sign, people were happy to donate, and the kids raised more than $80 in just a few hours.

Continuing the Battle

Meanwhile, in India, the clubs Jyoti started are making a small but important difference, and change is coming slowly for India's young women and children. Recently, for example, a law was passed to give women more political power. It guarantees that one-third of all elected seats in local governing groups must be reserved for women.

Women such as these are making strides in many male-dominated areas, including business.

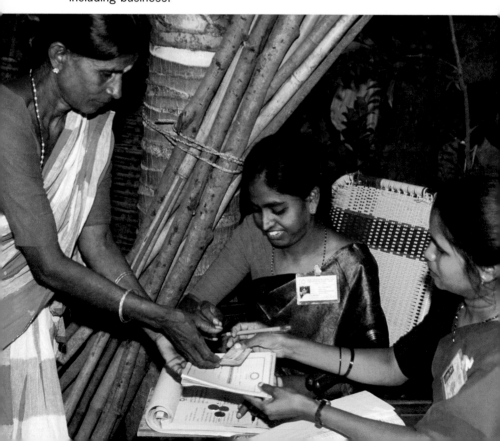

Even with such laws, however, it will be difficult to change long-held traditions, such as the belief that Indian women are second-class citizens who should stay in the home. This tradition is especially strong in rural parts of the country. Journalist Jasjit Kaur comments, "A change, almost revolutionary, is required in the mind-set of people, especially in traditional and rural India where even the women cannot appreciate the idea of being equal to a man."[17]

The Meena Clubs have already accomplished many things. They have helped improve heath care, reduce abuse cases, promote good parenting, and aid communication between children and adults in their region of India. In the future, the Meena Girls plan to start campaigns to reduce infant deaths, ban child labor, and give all children proper educational chances.

Changing such big issues will be very difficult, of course. However, small victories can lead to larger ones, and the Meena Girls have set their goals high. Reporter Manoj Kar writes, "Thousands of Meenas and leaders like Jyoti know they can hardly remain content with small little islands of success."[18]

The Future

Jyoti hopes to see the concept of the Meena Club spread in the future. She would like to see clubs that are already established help new groups get started. However, she says that most of the work must come from members of the new clubs, because she strongly believes that people must help themselves. Jyoti comments, "When people

One of Jyoti's goals is to help increase educational opportunities for all children.

from different villages ask me to come and establish a Meena Club, I tell them they need to start one themselves, and then I will visit and work with them."[19]

And Jyoti wants to expand the Meena Club's reach. In fact, she hopes to take the message of youth activism around the world. She says, "I would like to see more and more young people as youth leaders, working for a caring and friendly society."[20]

However, there is much still to be done, not just in India but everywhere. All over the world, millions of girls and women—and boys and men—are hungry or unhappy or abused. Jyoti says simply, "The battle has just begun."[21]

As for her personal plans, Jyoti is currently a postgraduate student in political science. And she has a big dream. She hopes to lead her country's government in the future: "Someday, I want to be India's prime minister."[22] With the brains, good fortune, and determination Jyoti has so far shown, she is well on her way.

Notes

Chapter 1: Introducing Jyoti

1. Quoted in http://66.102.7.104/
   search?q=cache:lzg4fogmnTcJ:mactest.
   cidercone.com/opencms/opencms/
   makeaconnection/org/content/Publications/
   pdf/yan_handbook_2004.pdf+%22We+believe
   +that+unity+is+our+strength,%22+&hl=en.

2. Quoted in Pradip Kumar Mohapatra,
   "Introduction to MEENA," August 7,
   2002, reprinted on [Ornet] Introduction to
   Meena, https://lists.cs.columbia.edu/
   pipermail/ornet/2002-August/005093.html.

3. Quoted in https://lists.cs.columbia.edu/
   pipermail/ornet/2002-August/005093.html.

4. Quoted in Sheila Kinkade and Christina
   Macy, *Our Time Is Now: Young People
   Changing the World.* Baltimore: Pearson
   Foundation/International Youth
   Foundation, 2005, p. 155.

5. Quoted in International Youth Foundation,
   "Perspectives on Children and Youth,"
   January 10, 2005, reprinted on *Youth On
   Children,* http://66.102.7.104/search?q=
   cache:6iMRG_uhXi0J:www.iyfnet.org/
   uploads/PERSPECTIVES1204.pdf+%22
   Some+day,+I+want+to+be+India%E2%80
   %99s+prime+minister.%22&hl=en.

6. Quoted in Kinkade and Macy, p. 158.

Chapter 2: The Problems
7. Quoted in Kinkade and Macy, pp. 156–57.

Chapter 3: The Meena Club Is Born
8. Quoted in Manoj Kar, "Social activist wins international award,"September 24, 2004, NDTV.com, reprinted on NDTV.com News, http://ndtv.com/morenews/showmorestory. asp?id=60939.
9. Quoted in Kinkade and Macy, p. 158.
10. Quoted in "Orissa Village Girl Bags Global Youth Award," Rediff.com, India online news service, October 15, 2004, http:// www.rediff.com/news/2004/oct/15oris.htm.

Chapter 4: Work for the Future
11. Quoted in International Youth Foundation, "Perspectives on Children and Youth," January 10, 2005, reprinted on *Youth On Children,* http://66.102.7.104/search?q= cache:6iMRG_uhXi0J:<url</url>>www.iyf net.org/uploads/PERSPECTIVES1204.pdf+ %22Some+day,+I+want+to+be+India%E2 %80%99s+prime+minister.%22&hl=en.
12. Quoted in International Youth Foundation, "Perspectives on Children and Youth," January 10, 2005, reprinted on *Youth On Children,* http://66.102.7.104/search?q=

cache:6iMRG_uhXi0J:www.iyfnet.org/uploads/PERSPECTIVES1204.pdf+%22Some+day,+I+want+to+be+India%E2%80%99s+prime+minister.%22&hl=en.

13. Quoted in "Orissa Village Girl Bags Global Youth Award."

14. Quoted in "Orissa Village Girl Bags Global Youth Award."

15. Quoted in Kinkade and Macy, p. 159.

16. Quoted in Kinkade and Macy, p. 155.

17. Jasjit Kaur, "India: Gender: The Inequality," Businessline, October 29, 2001, p. 1, reprinted on http://wf2la3.webfeat. org:80/.

18. Quoted in Manoj Kar, "Social Activist Wins International Award," NDTV.com, http://ndtv.com/morenews/showmorestory.asp?id=60939.

19. Quoted in http://66.102.7.104/search?q=cache:6iMRG_uhXi0J:www.iyfnet.org/uploads/PERSPECTIVES1204.pdf+%22Some+day,+I+want+to+be+India%E2%80%80%99s+prime+ minister.%22&hl=en.

20. Quoted in Kincade and Macy, "Youth in Action: Profiles of Youth Leading Change Around the World," Youth Action Network, reprinted on Cover of *YAN Handbook3A.indd,* http://66.102.7.104/search?q=cache:lzg4foGmnTcJ:mactest.

cidercone.com/opencms/opencms/makea
connection/org/content/Publications/pdf/
yan_handbook_2004.pdf+%22WE+believe
+that+unity+is+our+strength,%22+&hl=en.

21. Quoted in "Orissa Village Girl Bags
Global Youth Award."

22. Quoted in Kincade and Macy, http://66.
102.7.104/search?q=cache:6iMRG_uhXi0J:
www.iyfnet.org/uploads/PERSPECTIVES12
04.pdf+%22Some+day,+I+want+to+be+
India%E2%80%99s+prime+minister.%22
&hl=en.

Glossary

activists: People who work for social change.

bride torture: The practice in rural India of abusing a bride to get money from her parents.

child abuse: Cruel treatment. Abuse can be physical, mental, or sexual.

child labor: The practice of putting children to hard work at very young ages.

child marriage: The practice of marrying children at very young ages.

chronic: Continuing over a long period of time.

cyclone (also called a **typhoon**): A powerful storm that comes twice yearly in certain parts of the world.

dowry: An illegal but widely accepted custom in India of a bride's family paying money or goods to the groom.

fertilizer: Material, often chemicals, used to help plants grow.

illiterate: Unable to read or write.

mentor: Someone who acts as a guide or teacher.

pesticide: Material, often chemicals, used to keep insects from eating crops.

poverty: The condition of being extremely poor.

rural: In the country, away from the city.

sanitation: Public cleanliness.

For Further Exploration

Books

Lee Engfer, *India in Pictures*. Minneapolis: Lerner, 2003. An excellent visual introduction to Jyoti's country, its joy as well as its sadness.

Sheila Kinkade and Christina Macy, *Our Time Is Now: Young People Changing the World*. Baltimore: Pearson Foundation/International Youth Foundation, 2005. This book has a series of profiles of youth activists, including Jyoti Mohapatra, and nice photos.

Patricia J. Murphy, *India*. New York: Bench-mark, 2003. A clearly written introduction to the country.

Magazine articles

(no author given) "Interview: Jyotirmahee (Jyoti) Mohapatra." *Perspectives on Children and Youth*, December 2004. Reprinted on http://72.14.203.104/ search?q=cache:6iMRG_uhXi0J:www.iyfnet. org/uploads/PERSPECTIVES1204.pdf+%22 Perspectives+on+Children+and+Youth%22+ jyoti&hl=en&gl=us&ct=clnk&cd=1.

Web sites

"Welcome to Meena's World." This site for
   kids is maintained by UNICEF and is all
   about Meena. http://www.unicef.org/meena/.
"Voices of Youth." The official site for
   UNICEF's organization Voices of Youth,
   which promotes activism among young
   people. http://www.unicef.org/voy/index.php.

Index

Picture Credits

About the Author

Adam Woog has written many books for adults, young adults, and children. He lives in his hometown, Seattle, Washington, with his wife and daughter.